Robert Ingpen

The Age of Acorns

Copyright © 1988 Robert Ingpen

First published 1988 by
Lothian Publishing Company Pty Ltd,
Melbourne, Australia

This edition published 1990 by Blackie and Son Ltd
7 Leicester Place
London WC2 7BP

British Library Cataloguing in Publication Data
Ingpen, Robert, 1936–
    The age of acorns.
    I. Title
    823 [J]
    ISBN 0-216-93009-X

First American edition published in 1990 by
Peter Bedrick Books,
2112 Broadway, New York, N.Y. 10023
Copyright © 1988 Robert Ingpen

All rights reserved.
Published by agreement with
Lothian Publishing Co Pty Ltd, Australia

Library of Congress Cataloging-in-Publication Data
Ingpen, Robert R.
    The age of acorns.
    Summary: When his human family leaves him up a
tree after a day of play, Bear reflects on past
adventures as he waits to be rescued.
    [1. Teddy bears — Fiction] I. Title.
PZ7.1534 Ag 1990   [E]   90-433
ISBN 0-87226-436-X

Printed in Hong Kong

Blackie
London

Bedrick/Blackie
New York

Bear was deep in thought.

The Others had sat him high in the old oak tree to be what they called 'a lookout'. He had been told to watch out for dragons, and that was just what he had been doing during the game.

Being deep in thought was the thing he most liked to do. Thinking is what a bear like him does best. He was so good at thinking after many years of practice that he could pretend to be doing something else at the same time. The Others — the children who made up the games — never knew what he was thinking about.
But they knew he was thinking.

It was the end of summer. Bear was thinking deeply about how good it would be if summer could last all the year. Now was the time he liked most of all. The time when most happened in the garden around the old oak tree. For Bear it was the Age of Acorns.

The acorns that formed among the green oak leaves around his lookout branch had begun to turn brown and to loosen from their cups. Every now and then an early one would fall through the canopy of leaves and go 'plop' on the garden far below.

Summer would become autumn when all the acorns fell to the ground. Next, the leaves would change their green to brown and then fall. The tree would be bare, and it would be winter.

And, thought Bear, if the Others didn't soon remember to fetch him to take him inside he might have to stay in the tree while all that happened around him.

Sometime earlier the Others had been called into the house for tea. Usually he would have been gathered up and taken inside. But that evening he had been left behind, and would have to remain where he was until someone remembered him.

Even as it grew dark Bear could still see the house where the Others had gone. He could hear their chatter and the sounds of tea.

There were always four children who played the games that needed him, two who lived in the house, and two who came from up the street.

Once Bear had heard one of the children say that any good game had to have a bear in it. So he felt needed and important. But now it was becoming cold and dark, and Bear felt forgotten as he looked down through the leaves and gloom into the garden.

He looked in the direction of the back fence and could just see the walnut tree in the corner where 'The Nasties' came under the fence with their tanks and bombs and things, when it suited the Others. Along one side of the garden, beyond the clothes line and lavender hedge, was a cherry plum tree and an artichoke forest. Then, beyond that, were the Woods, the strange world of next door.

Bear felt sure one of the Others would come to fetch him as an excuse to get out of doing homework, or at the last moment between teeth-time and bed-time. Otherwise he would have to stay outside all night, and strange things happen in the garden at night. He knew that.

So, being a thinker, he tried not to think forward, and thought backwards. He thought about the game of Castles and Dragons that had been played in the usual way that afternoon. From his lookout place in the highest turret of the castle he could still imagine most of the battlefield. In his own special way he thought that he could see the retreating enemy through the smoke haze of cannon fire that wafted around the fortress walls.

Bear knew the enemy well. They had attacked many times after school during earlier ages of acorns. The Others knew them as dragons, and Bear supposed this was because they couldn't see what they were from his point of view. He could make them be any enemy he wanted them to be. He supposed that was why he was always given the part of Lookout-in-Games.

That afternoon, as usual, the dragons had been defeated. The weary knights and maidens had gone inside, and the smoke of battle began to smell like burning acorns in the incinerator near the back gate.

Night settled gently around the forgotten bear like reality after a dream. Bear tried not to think of the night, but further ahead to tomorrow. He guessed, as best he could, about what game the Others would choose to play after school tomorrow. If it was to be Pirates and Galleons there would be planks to walk. It might be Cowboys and Indians with arrows and scalpings and lots of noise. It could even be the game of Space Flights to Far Galaxies and he would do his special space walk.

Bear chose the Pirate Game to think about. The Others would raise 'The Jolly Roger' on the highest branch, and the tree would instantly become a pirate ship. There would be wooden swords and black eyepatches, and a treasure of golden acorns wrapped in silver paper to bury. Later, captives would be taken and teased with live beetles in matchboxes. Then he, the crow's nest lookout bear, would be taken down and tied up and made to walk the plank.

The game was always the same, and Bear knew his part in it like the back of his paw. It was the way of pirates' play.

Returning from thought, he noticed that it was quite dark. He could not see all the house, only the lights in some windows. Two lights downstairs, and one in the big bedroom upstairs, the one he should now be sharing with the rest of the toys belonging to the Others.

He thought about the house. From the outside it was two-storied, but inside in its rooms Bear knew of many stories. Just like me, Bear thought wisely. On the outside, just one thoughtful bear, but inside him somewhere is a whole lot of things he can think about, and remember, and forget, and even make up.

Outside the safety of the house strange things can happen in the garden at night. Strangers with unfamiliar games can use the garden for play while you sleep. Another world can come to visit.

Bear shivered a little shake that he copied from the children. The kind you make when you think of something scary. The shiver you do when pretending to be cold not frightened.

Bear shivered because he thought he saw a light in the artichoke forest by the fence that divided his world from where the

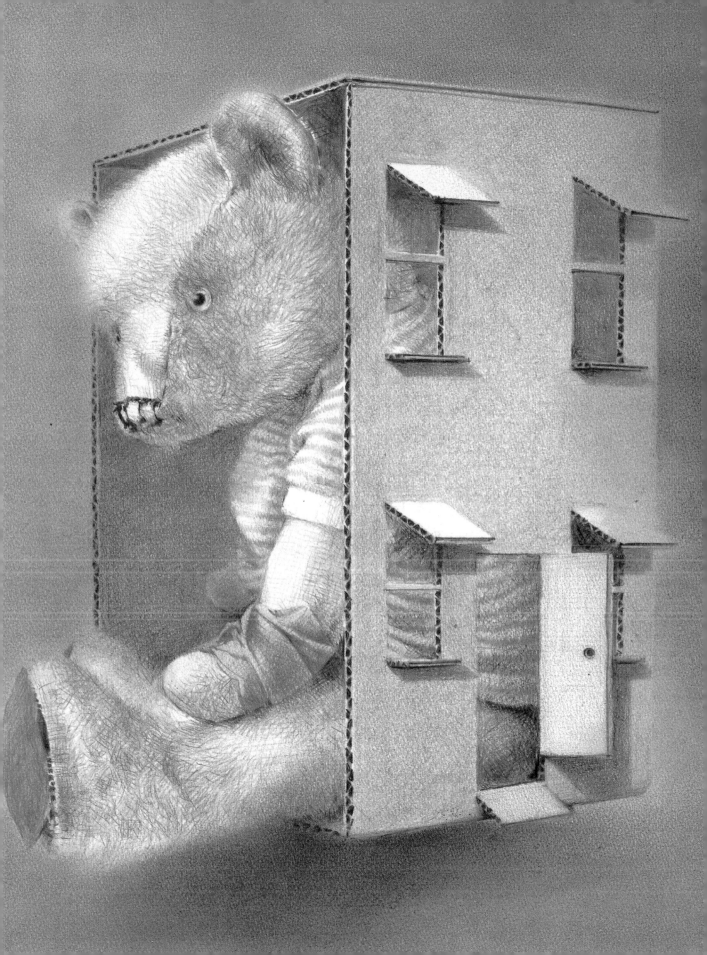

Woods family lived. The strange light danced about as if carried by somebody he couldn't see. He watched it weave its way around the clothes hung out on the line, then through the lavender hedge and out on the open garden. He watched it come to rest below his branch in the old oak tree.

Just then the moon appeared from behind a cloud to give him more light to see. And there they were! Four creatures stood in a group around the light directly below him. He clearly saw an old wrinkled woman dressed in green oak leaves that seemed to be sown on her like a patchwork quilt. She was holding a white lily which produced the scary yellow light. And she was pointing directly at him!

Beside her was Michael the sad dog who belonged to the Woods family. Beside him crouched Modestine the calculating cat. She also belonged to the Woods, when she wasn't away wandering.

The fourth member of the group was Belladonna Snagglefang. Bear had heard the Others talk of her but, until now, he had never seen her. She had been made by one of the Woods family out of old sacks, rope and bright paint. Her long body was stuffed full of wheat husks which spilt on the ground leaving a trail as she moved. She was looking up at him. They were all looking up at him!

Bear knew this was no game he had ever played before. It was something new, and he was frightened. They made no sound at all, and all the games he knew made sounds.

He wasn't really scared of Michael the sad dog or Modestine the cat because, until now, they had never shown much interest in a bear like him. But he felt quite unsure of the ugly doll Belladonna. She moved about as if she was alive, yet her painted face remained a fixed stare.

The sight of the old woman in green was the thing that gave him fear. She was clearly the one in control of whatever game they were about to play.

Then she spoke. 'Bear,' she cackled, 'Bear, down you be coming. We have a game, a new game, to teach you. Down you be coming, Bear.' And her voice tailed off to a fearful laugh.

The next thought that Bear had was so tightly squashed between fear on each side that it was hardly a thought at all. For, as she had spoken he had seen her teeth. They were green! Green as the leaves that made the clothes she wore. Instantly he knew that she must be Jenny Greenteeth the Story Witch. And she was in his garden, his world.

Until now Jenny Greenteeth had only appeared in a story. One called *Giantland* which was sometimes read to the Others by somebody in the Woods family.

A scary story to be told only when the children were safely tucked into bed inside the house.

Bear and the other toys pretended not to be listening to the tales told of that evil witch. That's what toy corners in children's bedrooms are for.
For overhearing stories. He had always been sure she was too evil ever to come out of a story and be real. But now he could see he had been wrong.

She beckoned to him as only witches can. With a long twiggy finger which seemed to have green slime dangling from it, she beckoned him down from his familiar place high in the tree.

He watched the slimy finger in the lily light and the moon, and felt himself moving to obey her command. He had never ever done that before, he thought, as he moved to get up. He'd never actually moved without help before.

Bear trembled unsteadily as he reached down for the branch below, and then the next.

Then there came a familiar sound, a comforting sound that often broke up the games the Others played. The back door of the house was opened and somebody he knew was coming at last to bring him inside.

They had remembered him. He was no longer forgotten. As he waited now to be rescued he looked down again at the terrible group. A cloudlike mist had begun to swirl around to hide them. The kind of mist, he thought, in which anything might happen — where nothing is, but thinking makes it so.

And they just faded away altogether.

Safely inside the house, comfortable now in his corner with the other toys, Bear was still shivering. Not a pretended or copied one, but one of his very own. He was thinking about what had happened, and what might have happened in the garden that night.

And he is still thinking about it.